LAZY TOWN ™

Who Took the Cake?

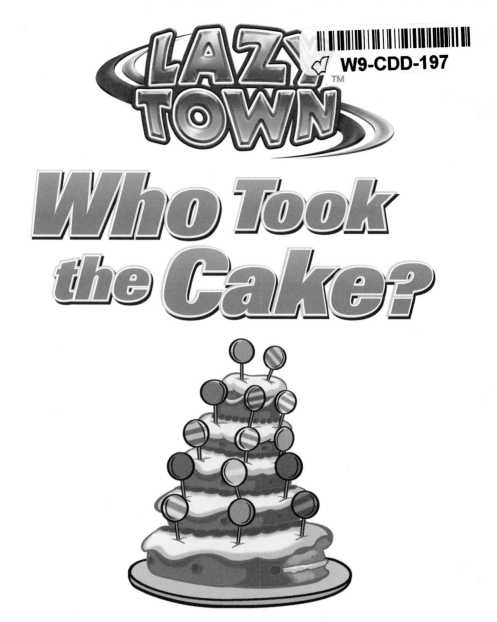

adapted by Zoey Zucker • based on the original teleplay by Magnús Scheving,
Noah Zachary, Cole Louie, Tom K. Mason, and Dan Danko
illustrated by Mark Marderosian and Mike Giles

Ready-to-Read

SIMON SPOTLIGHT/NICK JR.
New York   London   Toronto   Sydney

Based on the TV series *LazyTown*™ as seen on Nick Jr.®

SIMON SPOTLIGHT
An imprint of Simon & Schuster Children's Publishing Division
1230 Avenue of the Americas, New York, New York 10020
Manufactured in the United States of America
First Edition
2 4 6 8 10 9 7 5 3 1
Library of Congress Cataloging-in-Publication Data
Zucker, Zoey.
Who took the cake?/adapted by Zoey Zucker; story by Magnus Scheving and Mani Svavarsson;
illustrated by Mark Marderosian and Mike Giles.
p. cm.–(Ready-to-read)
"Based on the teleplay, "Swiped Sweets" by Noah Zachary, Cole Louie, Tom K. Mason, and Dan Danko."
"Based on the TV series LazyTown created by Magnus Scheving as seen on Nick Jr."
ISBN-13: 978-1-4169-0694-0
ISBN-10: 1-4169-0694-0
I. Scheving, Magnus. II. Svavarsson, Mani. III. Marderosian, Mark ill. IV. LazyTown (Television program)
V. Title. VI. Series.
PZ7.Z77958Who 2006
[E]–dc22
2005025466

STEPHANIE , PIXEL , ZIGGY ,

and STINGY are making

a CAKE for BESSIE 's

birthday.

The  is done!
CAKE

ZIGGY puts LOLLIPOPS on top.

"What a pretty  !"
CAKE

says  .
THE MAYOR

"But I will make it look

like
SPORTACUS
took the ."
CAKE

 calls  .

THE MAYOR   BESSIE

"Happy birthday!" says

 . "Come over

THE MAYOR

and open your  ."

GIFT

But sneaks in

ROBBIE ROTTEN

and takes the .

CAKE

Then  eats

ROBBIE ROTTEN

the 🎂! Some

CAKE

LOLLIPOPS

fall off the 🎂.

CAKE

BESSIE comes and

opens her GIFT.

"The CAKE is not here,"

says THE MAYOR.

"Who took the cake?"

"We can find out

who took the ,"

CAKE

says .

PIXEL

STEPHANIE , ZIGGY , PIXEL , and

 STINGY go out.

They see SPORTACUS 's AIRSHIP .

They find  ...

SPORTACUS

. . . with frosting on his  !

HANDS

"Look!" says  .
STINGY

"I think  took the
SPORTACUS   CAKE

and ate the  !"
CAKE

"I did not take the ,
CAKE

and I did not eat the ,"
CAKE

says . "Look."
SPORTACUS

does **10** sit-ups.
SPORTACUS   TEN

"Sugar makes  sleepy,"

SPORTACUS

says  . "So  did not

PIXEL   SPORTACUS

eat the  !"

CAKE

STEPHANIE , ZIGGY , PIXEL ,

and STINGY still want

to find out who took

the CAKE .

ZIGGY finds some LOLLIPOPS .

The LOLLIPOPS lead to ROBBIE ROTTEN .

" ROBBIE ROTTEN took the CAKE !"

says PIXEL .

ZIGGY , PIXEL , STINGY , and

STEPHANIE make a new 🎂 .

CAKE

They put 🍭 on top.

LOLLIPOPS

calls  .

THE MAYOR   BESSIE

"Come over!" says .

THE MAYOR

"We have a new

GIFT

for you!"

has a happy birthday.

BESSIE

This time

ROBBIE ROTTEN

does not take the  !

CAKE